Bring a Torch, Jeanette Isabella

Bring a Torch,
Jeanette Isabella

Tamela Baker

For my father

1995

Jean-Jacques Broussard was a most honorable man by all accounts.

Nobody knew exactly how much Broussard was worth, but most of the residents of Chateau-St. Gregoire depended on him for their livelihoods, working in one or another of his various enterprises. Those who did not, well, they were dependent on those who did.

Nevertheless Broussard was an unassuming man, choosing to live in a modest home among those of his employees, spending his Saturdays watching the children play ball, giving away much of his money to hospitals, schools, churches. Children were especially fond of him; he could be counted on to tell them stories and dispense trinkets for no apparent reason. He had been at the center of Chateau-St. Gregoire forever, it seemed, and nobody ever thought to ask him why he had never married or why he walked with that cane; why he lit Hanukkah candles every winter even though he wasn't Jewish or why he always wore long sleeves, even in summer. He was their gentle benefactor, as familiar as the decaying fortress from which the village took its name.

He was the special friend of Alexandre and Lisette Villon, who lived in the house just next to his on the Rue Louis Roi. And that was a good thing, because 7-year-old Alexandre was in special need of a friend.

Alexandre hadn't meant to get into any trouble. And just now he couldn't remember whether it was he or Marc who started the water fight in the boys' room at school, but he was quite certain it must have been Marc. And naturally, Alexandre had been obliged to respond. Soon both boys were soaked, the floor was flooded, and Alexandre had discovered how to block the spigot just enough to aim the spray right at Marc's nose. And in one incredible second, the stream arced, Marc ducked, the door opened, and the wave crashed all over the trousers of the man standing in the doorway. Marc and Alexandre looked up, up into the blazing eyes of Monsieur Robichot, the headmaster.

Now Monsieur Robichot's parting words thundered in Alexandre's mind as he slowly made his way home from school. *I will decide your punishment tomorrow.* Alexandre couldn't guess what Monsieur Robichot would do to him, and now he had the whole night to worry about it.

He absently dragged a stick along the wrought iron rail lining the sidewalk. Maybe Maman wouldn't find out. He hoped not. Whatever terror Monsieur Robichot devised wouldn't compare to the tribulation that awaited him when Maman meted out her own discipline.

Alexandre heard someone trailing behind him, jolting him back to the present. He turned to see Jean-Jacques Broussard following him, dragging his cane along the rail, mimicking Alexandre.

"Bonjour, Monsieur Broussard," Alexandre said without conviction.

"Bonjour, Monsieur Villon. What troubles you, my friend?" Alexandre glanced back at Broussard. *How did he know?*

"Did something happen at school today?"

With Monsieur Broussard's reassuring arm about his slender shoulders, Alexandre poured out his troubles, carefully placing the bulk of responsibility for his plight squarely on Marc.

"I told Monsieur Robichot I was sorry," he wailed. "What do you think he will do?"

"Tell me, Alexandre, why did you tell Monsieur Robichot you were sorry?"

"Well … I guess …" Well, to be honest, Alexandre hadn't really thought about that.

"Was it because you didn't want to be punished?"

"Yes …"

"And not because you knew what you had done was wrong?"

Alexandre looked up at his friend, not quite grasping where this conversation was going.

"You knew when you and Marc were playing that you would be punished if you were caught, didn't you?"

"Well, yes, if we got caught …"

"And if you hadn't been caught, it still wouldn't have been the best thing for you to do, would it?"

"I guess not."

"Well then." Monsieur Broussard chuckled. "You know, Alexandre, there will always be choices to make. And you will have decide whether to do the things you know are right, or the things you know are wrong. You must always choose to do the right thing, Alexandre, though you may sometimes get into trouble even for that. The right choices may not always be the easy ones, but they will always be the right ones. Do you understand?"

"I think so. You won't tell Maman, will you?"

"Oh no. But you must."

"I can't! Monsieur Broussard …"

"Alexandre, Alexandre … don't you think telling your mother would be the right thing to do?"

Alexandre hadn't expected to be tested so quickly. A moment ago Monsieur Broussard was just giving advice. Now Alexandre was expected to take it.

"I think it will go much easier for you if *you* tell her than if she hears about this from Monsieur Robichot," Monsieur Broussard cautioned.

"Alexandre! There you are! Why are you so late? I was about to come looking for you!"

Madeleine Villon waved from her gate. Four-year-old Lisette peeped through the rail. "Bonjour, Monsieur Broussard!" Lisette chirped.

"Bonjour, Mademoiselle Lisette. Forgive me, Madame Villon. You know I walk rather slowly, and Alexandre has been keeping me company."

"There is no need, Monsieur Broussard," Madeleine laughed. "Had I known he was with you, I wouldn't have worried. Alexandre, come inside. I have some things for you to do before Papa gets home."

Broussard fished two caramels from his pocket and handed them to Alexandre. "One of these is for your sister. *Bon chance*," he whispered, and was gone.

"You are certain this is Erich Braun?" François Fournier stared at the documents his deputy minister had assembled.

"Reasonably. But we need a decision from you to go forward with prosecution."

"Extradition …?"

"I've already started proceedings."

"When can we expect him?"

"By November, I'm sure."

"If I give you authority to go ahead with this, you must be absolutely certain you have the right man and that you have sufficient evidence against him. I want every possible witness in that courtroom, Gastineau. I won't take this to trial unless I know we'll get a conviction. If we lose this case we'll have every Jew in France on our backs."

"I understand, sir. But I think the reaction we have if we lose will not compare with the one we will have if we do not go to trial at all."

Fournier considered that; he knew Gastineau was right, but he still felt uneasy. "I'll let you know when I've decided," he finally said.

"Sir, could you give me a decision now?" Annoyed, Fournier glanced up at his aide. "It's only that the witnesses are very old, sir. We must proceed while they're still … with us."

Fournier glared at Claude Gastineau for a moment. Another valid point. "All right," Fournier said at last. "Go ahead."

"Thank you, sir." Gastineau started for the door.

"Claude …"

"Yes sir?"

"Leave nothing undone."

"Yes sir."

Fournier sat alone in his Justice Ministry office, studying the worn photo of a young Nazi officer. "Will that war ever be over?" he muttered.

From her bedroom window, Lisette Villon could see Jean-Jacques Broussard, rake in hand, working in his garden. It was, it seemed, a perfect time for a visit. Soon she was down the stairs and out the door to get a closer look at what her old friend was doing.

In this private place, Broussard had rolled up his shirtsleeves, and, leaning heavily on the rake, had begun clearing out the overgrowth from the summer. He didn't notice Lisette until she appeared at his side. "What are you doing, Monsieur Broussard?" she inquired.

"Hello, Lisette. I'm clearing out the dead plants so that in spring, the new ones will have room to grow."

"Can I try?"

"Of course." He guided her tiny hands along the rake, and helped her tug at the dead plants until they slid out of the earth. "See how strong you are, Lisette? You're doing very well."

She giggled and pulled harder, and more of the spent roots

emerged. She looked up and grinned, but then reached for Broussard's elbow and began to examine it. "Monsieur Broussard," she asked, "why did you write that number on your arm?"

Broussard stiffened a little. "Someone else did that, Lisette. A long time ago."

"Why?"

"So that I wouldn't get lost, I suppose."

"Did they do that at your school?"

"No, no. It was a sort of camp."

"Why don't you wash it off?"

Broussard smiled. "I've tried," he said, rolling down his sleeves and buttoning the cuffs. "It doesn't come off."

"Look, Maman! I'm helping Monsieur Broussard make his flowers grow!" Lisette called to her mother, who was headed to Jean-Jacques' garden to retrieve her.

"Oh yes, Lisette, I'm sure you're helping Monsieur Broussard a great deal," Madeleine said, taking Lisette's hand. "You mustn't bother Monsieur Broussard while he's working …"

"Oh no, Madame," Jean-Jacques protested. "Lisette has been working very hard."

"Yes, Monsieur Broussard, I saw how hard she was working," Madeleine laughed. "By the way, I want to thank you for persuading Alexandre to tell me about his trouble at school last week."

"How did he fare with Monsieur Robichot? He was most concerned about that …"

"He has to stay after school every day next week. It's not unreasonable, but it's a little inconvenient for us. We're going to have to juggle some things so I can get to the school to pick him up; I don't want him walking home so late alone."

"I can help you with that, Madame Villon. I must go to Marseille on Monday, but if you can manage that day, I'll be happy to stop by the school and collect him for the rest of the week."

"I couldn't impose Alexandre on you, Monsieur Broussard …"

"Madame, your children are never an imposition."

Madeleine announced her arrangement with Broussard during dinner that evening. "You must be sure to thank Monsieur Broussard for his trouble, Alexandre. He'll have to go out of his way to get to the school."

"Maman, did you know the number on Monsieur Broussard's arm won't come off?" Lisette asked.

"The number on his arm?"

"Mmmhmm. He said somebody put it on there a long time ago and it won't come off."

Madeleine and her husband exchanged startled glances. Now both children were looking to Madeleine for an answer. "No, Lisette," she said, "I've never seen it. Finish your dinner before it gets cold."

After the children were in bed she asked her husband if he knew what had happened to Broussard during the war.

"No idea," Alain replied. "In the 10 years I've worked for him, I don't think I've ever heard it discussed."

"I wonder why he would have been interned. He's not Jewish, or gypsy …"

"He must have done something to annoy the Nazis; I suspect it didn't take very much."

"No, I suppose not," Madeleine replied, and let the matter drop.

Every Sunday morning the routine was the same. First an invocation, then Monsieur Broussard would read Scripture, then a hymn and another prayer and Pastor Duvalier would speak. And Alexandre's mind would drift miles away from the church.

Today he had brought along a more tangible diversion—a small rubber ball he was happily tossing in the air while everyone else's heads were bowed for prayer and he assumed nobody was looking. That is until he heard Monsieur Broussard's uneven step as he made his way to the front of the sanctuary for the Scripture reading. Alexandre cupped the ball in his hand and bowed his own head as Monsieur Broussard passed by. Then he resumed his little game of catch, tossing the ball higher and higher—until it

slipped through his fingers to the floor. Alexandre watched help-
lessly as it rolled down the aisle where Monsieur Broussard was
walking. Monsieur Broussard stopped it with his foot, picked
it up and dropped it into his pocket. When the prayer ended,
Monsieur Broussard began to read:

"From the 51st Psalm:

"Have mercy upon me, O God, According to Your lovingkind-
ness; According to the multitude of Your tender mercies, Blot out
my transgressions.

"Wash me thoroughly from my iniquity, And cleanse me from
my sin.

"For I acknowledge my transgressions, And my sin is always
before me …."

Alexandre felt his heart thumping against his ribs. He was in
trouble again. What would Monsieur Broussard say to him this
time? Worse yet, would Monsieur Broussard tell Maman? Or
would he have to tell her himself?

Monsieur Broussard finished reading the psalm and settled
into a seat right behind Alexandre. And all through the service,
Alexandre was keenly aware of Monsieur Broussard's presence.
He thought he could feel Monsieur Broussard watching him,
taking into account every breath. He tried not to squirm too
much, even when Lisette fell asleep on his elbow. Until today,
he'd never really noticed how long the service could last.

When it was finally over and everyone started to leave, Alexandre felt Monsieur Broussard's firm grip on his shoulder as he chatted with Maman; and there was something else—his rubber ball, hidden in Monsieur Broussard's palm. Alexandre slid his own hand under Monsieur Broussard's and retrieved the toy, and managed to hide it in his pocket without Maman noticing.

Outside, Alexandre spied Monsieur Broussard headed out of the churchyard, and, feeling oddly penitent, ran to catch him.

"Monsieur Broussard …"

"Yes, Alexandre?"

"Monsieur Broussard, I won't bring it to church any more. I promise."

Jean-Jacques smiled. "It wasn't the best thing to do, was it?"

"No … I won't do it again, I prom-"

"Oh I believe you, Alexandre."

"Thank you for not telling Maman."

"Well, since no one else saw it, we'll let it be our secret this time. You'd better get back now; your maman will be looking for you."

On Monday Jean-Jacques Broussard finished his business in Marseille and, as was his habit, purchased a copy of *Le Monde* at the train station to read on his way home. He chose a seat near the door and settled in, scanning the headlines above the fold and then flipping the paper over to see what else was on the front page.

And there among the jumble of crime and politics was the face that had haunted him for decades.

"Trial Set for Nazi War Crimes Suspect," the headline announced, and the caption under the old photo of Erich Braun noted that the man arrested in Canada claimed he wasn't Erich Braun at all.

The eyes in the photo seemed to fix on Broussard, just as they had before; cold and dark and relishing the helplessness they saw in him. Even now he could feel the man's fists pummeling his face; the boot in his stomach. He could see the odd triangular scar on the man's forearm as he gripped Broussard's throat.

For years he had wanted desperately to forget, and in his darker moments he hoped Erich Braun was dead. Now he felt his energy draining and he found it difficult to breathe.

"Pardon, monsieur ... monsieur?"

Broussard came out of his trance long enough to allow a young woman to reach a seat opposite him. As he sat back down he began to read the brief article, which said the Justice Ministry believed this man had deported thousands of French Jews during the occupation. He had fought extradition and lost, and now was pleading mistaken identity.

The Justice Ministry would have a difficult task, Broussard thought. Fifty years is a long time. So many things change.

Everything, of course, except the past.

"Bonjour, Madame. My name is Claude Gastineau and I am with the Justice Ministry. I need to speak with Monsieur Broussard. Is he in?"

"He is meeting with someone just now," said Broussard's assistant. "Is he expecting you?"

"I don't think so. May I wait for him? It's very important that I see him."

"Yes, if you wish; I will tell him you're here when he—Oh, Monsieur Broussard —"

Gastineau turned to see Broussard and another man entering the room. "This is Monsieur Gastineau from the Justice Ministry," the assistant continued. "He says he needs to speak with you ...."

"Monsieur Gastineau," Broussard said, extending his hand. "This is Alain Villon, one of our managers at Compagnie St. Gregoire. Alain, do you have enough to go on for now?"

"Yes, Monsieur Broussard. We can discuss the rest in the morning. Monsieur Gastineau." Villon nodded and left.

"Come into my office, Monsieur Gastineau," said Broussard, "and tell me what it is we need to talk about."

"Merci, Monsieur," Gastineau said, taking the seat Broussard offered. "You are renowned in Paris for your business sense and your generosity. I'm sorry we have not met before."

"You are very kind, Monsieur Gastineau. But I gather you did not come here today to compliment me on my contribution to the French economy."

"No, Monsieur, I did not." Gastineau hesitated for a moment; he hadn't imagined this conversation would be simple. And now he felt strangely inferior in the older man's presence. "I am told you served in the Underground during the occupation. Is that true?"

"Yes."

"And you falsified documents for Jews trying to leave the country? You helped them escape?"

"Yes." Gastineau waited for Broussard to say more, but Broussard simply stared back at him, waiting for the next question.

"I have also been told that you were arrested by Gestapo in 1943. Is this also true?"

"Yes."

"Did you at that time have any dealings with an SS officer named Erich Braun?"

Broussard smiled slowly. "Monsieur Gastineau, you are asking me to remember things I have been trying for half a century to forget. I trust you have a good reason for doing so."

"We believe we have found Erich Braun —"

"Yes, I know you do. The news reports were hard to miss. But what is your interest in me?"

"We're bringing him to trial, Monsieur Broussard, but he is claiming we have the wrong man. Do you think you could identify Erich Braun?"

"You want me for a witness against this man?"

"Can you identify him?"

Broussard studied Gastineau for a moment, then rose to his feet. "I want no part of this trial," he said, "I'm sorry."

"I don't understand. I should think that two years at Auschwitz would have been more than enough to make you want to bring this man to justice."

Broussard turned to face Gastineau. "Justice? Monsieur Gastineau, no court in France or anywhere else can bring justice for what happened then."

"I understand how you feel, Monsieur, but …"

"No, you do not understand, Monsieur Gastineau." Broussard smiled sadly. "You cannot possibly understand. And even if you have indeed found Erich Braun, you cannot restore what was lost by sending an old man to die in prison."

"But Monsieur Broussard," Gastineau said slowly, "wasn't that the fate he had planned for you?"

"Perhaps that is the difference between us," Broussard replied. "They did what they did because they could. I do not take responsibility for another man's life so lightly."

"Even if that other man is a murderer?"

Broussard glared at Gastineau. Neither man spoke for an excruciating moment. "I can compel you to testify, Monsieur Broussard," Gastineau finally managed. "But I'd rather not."

Broussard looked down at the floor. "That will not be necessary," he said. "Erich Braun had an unusual scar on his forearm—a sort of triangle, with the skin seared in the center."

Finally, something concrete. "Would you be able to recognize it if you saw it again?" Gastineau asked.

Broussard smiled. "I had a rather good look at it while he was choking me," he said. "You must excuse me now; I have promised to accompany a small boy home from school."

When he was alone that night, Jean-Jacques Broussard scanned his library for something to take his mind off the meeting with Claude Gastineau. Flaubert, Moliere; Dumas the elder, Dumas the younger … he finally settled on Hugo. Perhaps he could lose himself in someone's make-believe troubles long enough to forget about his own.

He hadn't been reading long, it seemed, when he thought he

heard a step behind him. As he looked around, he saw Claire. She was wearing a blue dress—he'd always liked her in blue—and she was smiling at him. She bent to kiss his cheek; just a whisper of a kiss. He reached to touch her hair, but his fingers grasped only air.

Dreaming. Again.

The only sound in the room was the clock ticking on the mantle. Broussard felt the ache surge from somewhere within him and spread until it engulfed the whole of him; so familiar and yet so fresh. The tick-tick-tick of the clock began to throb, mocking him with its numbing monotony. He crossed the room and looked into its face. "Stop," he said, as if it could obey a verbal command. "Stop!" He knocked the little clock to the floor and heard the crash, and then the silence. Leaning on his cane, he stared at its shattered remains. *That is my life*, he thought.

Claude Gastineau was anxious to pay a visit to his vexing prisoner. He found him to be predictably uncooperative, as he had been on all previous occasions. But today Gastineau was looking for more than conversation.

"I trust you are feeling well today, Monsieur Braun?"

"Steuben."

"Steuben. Forgive me. I keep forgetting. Are you getting all your medications?"

"With great difficulty. I usually have to ask several times for my insulin. I must have it every day; they know that."

"You inject that in your arm don't you?" Gastineau asked, sliding up the old man's sleeve. "You haven't had problems with the injections, have you? No swelling?"

"I take it in the other arm."

"Of course." Gastineau examined the prisoner's other arm. "No problems then?"

"I have problems getting it. I have never had problems with the medication itself, and I am surprised at your concern."

"I have no interest in seeing you get sick, Monsieur Steuben." Gastineau turned to leave. "I'll speak to the warden about getting you your medications."

"In return for what?"

"Nothing, Monsieur Steuben. In return for nothing."

Gastineau had seen all he needed to see. He returned to his office in better spirits than he had in weeks; he could finally tell Fournier he had no doubts about the man in the cell. He was just about to call Fournier when Philippe Legendre wandered in. "Sorry to just walk in like this, Claude," he said, "but your secretary wasn't at her desk and your door was open … may I trouble you for a moment?"

"You always trouble me."

Legendre laughed. "Good. That's what they pay me for."

Gastineau smiled. "What does *Le Monde* require from me today?"

"Just wanted to see where you were with Erich Braun. Have you set a trial date?"

"December 11 in Lyon."

"I can print that?"

"If you must."

"Can you win this one, Claude?"

"I wouldn't be going to trial if I didn't think I could win—"

"Excuse me, Monsieur Gastineau," said his secretary, appearing at the door. "Here's the file you asked for on Jean-Jacques Broussard."

"Broussard? Compagnie St.-Gregoire Jean-Jacques Broussard?" Legendre asked.

"He said he will arrange to be in Lyon when you need him," the secretary continued, "but he didn't seem very happy about it."

"Thank you, that will be all," Gastineau said, stopping her before she revealed anything else. She glanced nervously at Legendre and left.

"Broussard is a witness? What does a soft-spoken philanthropist have to do with a war criminal?"

"Leave it alone, Philippe."

"Should I pretend I didn't see that?"

"I'm counting on it. Philippe, you know I don't make a habit of keeping things from you. But I'm not Broussard's favorite person right now, and I need him. Don't make this harder than it is."

"He doesn't want to testify, then?"

"Forget it, Philippe."

"You're asking me to sit on a story."

Gastineau looked pleadingly at Legendre. "No I'm not," he said. "I'm asking you to help me make sure there *is* one."

Lisette accidentally stepped on Alexandre's foot during prayer. "Ow," he whispered. "Lisette, watch your feet!"

"Sorry," Lisette whispered back. Loudly. Alexandre caught a glimpse of Maman, one eye open, eyebrow raised, glaring at them. He quickly bowed his head.

At the front of the sanctuary, Monsieur Broussard began to read. He seemed a bit preoccupied, Pastor Duvalier thought, and was looking a little pale.

"From the Gospel of St. Matthew, chapter six:

"When you are praying, do not use meaningless repetition, as the Gentiles do, for they suppose that they will be heard for their many words. Therefore, do not be like them; for your Father knows what you need before you ask Him. Pray, then, in this way: Our Father who art in heaven, hallowed be Thy name. Thy kingdom come. Thy will be done, on earth as it is in heaven. Give us this day our daily bread. And forgive us our debts, as we also have forgiven our debtors."

Broussard pressed on as the words writhed in his throat. How *could* he forgive?

"And do not lead us into temptation, but deliver us from evil. For Thine is the kingdom, and the power, and the glory, forever. Amen.

"For if you forgive men for their transgressions, your heavenly Father will also forgive you. But if you do *not* forgive men, then your Father will not forgive your transgressions."

Broussard took his seat, drained by the implication of those words. Now it was *his* mind that wandered far from the church. He didn't even notice when Lisette peeked over the top of the pew and smiled.

He had known from the start what was expected of him. But didn't he have the right to hate Erich Braun? Couldn't God understand that?

On Dec. 10, Philippe Legendre left the Paris office of *Le Monde* and boarded a train for Lyon.

In Lyon, a crowd quietly gathered outside the *Palais de Justice*. Old men who remembered the occupation stood next to younger ones who demanded justice for relatives they had never had the chance to meet. From an upstairs window, François Fournier looked down on the scene and tried to ignore the tightening in his chest.

And in Chateau-St. Gregoire, Jean-Jacques Broussard purchased a single white rose and made his way to the cemetery, where, discarding the spent blossom from the week before, he carefully placed it on the headstone of Claire Delacroix.

For the first several days of the trial, Claude Gastineau had meticulously built his case against Erich Braun, with witness after witness describing in sickening detail what Braun had done during the nightmare years. It wasn't long before Philippe Legendre noticed he was no longer shocked by what he heard; the trial seemed to be falling into a routine. He wondered whether the judges felt the same way.

When he had filed his report after one particularly chronic session, Legendre went to a cafe near his hotel. There was no doubt in his mind that Erich Braun had been a monster. But he wasn't certain Claude was making much progress in proving the man on trial was really Erich Braun. The next day's session was the one

Legendre had been waiting for for weeks. Jean-Jacques Broussard was scheduled to testify, and his curiosity about Broussard's connection with Braun would finally be satisfied; though not as early as his editors would have liked. But Claude had set up roadblocks everywhere—nobody would talk to Legendre about Jean-Jacques Broussard. And every time he had tried to reach Broussard himself, he had been told Broussard was unavailable. He doubted Broussard was even aware that he wanted to talk to him.

His meal had just been served when he spotted Broussard walking into the cafe. This might be his only chance—tomorrow, everything would be complicated.

"Monsieur Broussard —"

Broussard looked around as he unbuttoned his coat. He recognized Legendre; he smiled faintly.

"Will you join me?"

The cafe was crowded, and to refuse would be impolite. Besides, he liked Legendre, and it had been a long time since they had last spoken. He draped his coat over an empty chair and sat down. "Please go on with your meal, Monsieur Legendre," he said. "It will get cold."

Legendre gestured to a waiter, who brought a menu to Broussard. "It has been too long, Monsieur Broussard," he said.

Broussard smiled. "I've wondered where you have been. Why are you no longer reporting on business?"

"The finance minister stopped speaking to me after that unfortunate bank strike."

"That was hardly your fault," Broussard laughed. "He couldn't very well keep something like that a secret."

"*You* tell him that."

"I will if I ever get the chance."

Broussard asked the waiter for coffee and a croissant. "What brings you to Lyon?" Legendre asked, feigning ignorance.

"I am on a sight-seeing excursion," Broussard replied.

Legendre smiled. "Sight-seeing at the *Palais de Justice?*"

Broussard eyed Legendre carefully. "A brief visit, I hope."

"Claude Gastineau seems most anxious to have you tell your story. And I confess that I'm most anxious to hear it." Broussard smiled, but betrayed nothing. "What happened during the war, Monsieur Broussard?" Legendre asked.

Broussard shrugged. "The world went mad," he said.

"You know that I'm asking what happened to *you*."

"Monsieur —"

"Philippe."

"Philippe. I'm not trying to be rude; it's only that I never discussed that with anyone until Claude Gastineau started asking questions, and I'm not sure I want to read about it in your paper."

"I can't imagine what harm there could be, unless … You surely weren't a collaborator …"

"I have been a Gaullist since 1940, Philippe."

"Well, you won't have a choice tomorrow; I'd rather give you the chance to tell your story now without being interrupted by defense attorneys."

Broussard's coffee arrived, and he let the warmth of it trickle down his throat. What Legendre said was quite true; there would be no choice tomorrow.

Jean-Jacques Broussard bristled as the wind sliced through his jacket. Pulling his collar tight, he glanced nervously around the dark wood to be sure he hadn't been followed.

Joel the tailor had chosen this remote farmhouse as a rendezvous point, but Jean-Jacques privately worried that it might be conspicuous by its very isolation. And tonight, the fresh snow wouldn't help. Who would make tracks in this place in the middle of the night? Still, any location in the village would expose more people to danger and suspicion; Jean-Jacques had reluctantly agreed. And so far they had been all right.

He quietly slid the barn door shut and stole across the field to the farmhouse. The door opened as he reached it, and Joel pulled him inside.

"You're late!"

"I had a little trouble getting out of St. Gregoire."

"Do you have their papers?"

"Yes. Where are they?"

"In the cellar with Claire."

"Where is Michel?"

"He's upstairs watching the road. The patrols are out here, too."

There were four of them in the cellar, frightened and cold, huddled in the light of a handful of candles. And there was Claire, relief softening her face as she clasped his shoulders. "I was beginning to worry, Jean," she whispered.

He squeezed her for a moment, but just a moment. He pulled a packet of documents from inside his jacket. "You are … ?" he said to one of the men.

"Matthieu Mandel."

"Not anymore." He handed Mandel a new passport, then distributed new passports to the others. "I didn't have time to get one for you, Joel, but I was promised there would be one waiting for you when we get to the border."

"For me? Why?"

"You're going this time, too."

"I cannot—there's too much to do here."

"It's too dangerous for you to stay, and Switzerland is closing up. You may not have another chance."

"Nonsense, Jean. They're only taking immigrant Jews. Like our friends here."

Jean-Jacques stared at Joel for a moment. "You haven't heard, then."

"Heard what?"

"They rounded up a whole group in Marseille last week—nationals like you. No Jew is safe anymore."

"Jean-Jacques—Joel. Come quickly," Michel called from the top of the stairs. They scrambled up the cellar steps and followed Michel to the top floor of the house. There the three of them peered through the window at a pair of approaching headlights. They held their breath as the dark sedan slowed. Finally it crawled past the house and up into the mountain.

"Gestapo?" Joel whispered.

"I'm sure of it," Jean-Jacques replied.

"Perhaps we shouldn't go tonight," Michel said.

"If we don't, how will we get word to the others?" Joel asked. "They're expecting us tonight."

"It's still snowing. Maybe it will cover our tracks," said Jean-Jacques. "If we don't go tonight, God knows when we'll be able to get out of here. They may freeze to death in the cellar."

They watched the sedan's lights until they disappeared.

"Michel, we'll try to fit everyone into your car. I'll drive behind you in mine," Jean-Jacques said. "Then if we're followed, I can distract them and you can go on."

"I'm going with you, Jean," said Joel.

"It's too dangerous …"

"We can't all fit in Michel's car. It's more important to get the younger ones out."

Jean-Jacques glared at Joel until Michel said "Let's go" and headed down the stairs.

In the barn, they squeezed everyone into Michel's car—everyone except Claire, who begged Jean-Jacques to let her go with him.

"You're safer with Michel," he said, but she wasn't listening. Finally he pulled her to him. "There's no time for this, Claire," he said. "I'll see you back in St. Gregoire in the morning. Everything will be all right; you'll see. But please—you have to do this for me."

He opened the passenger door wide and nudged her toward it. "Be sure to get back, Jean," she pleaded. "Please come back."

"I will. I promise." He kissed her, but she pulled away and climbed into the car. He closed the door as Michel turned the ignition. In the darkness, Jean-Jacques could just see her face through the window, lip quivering, hand pressed against the glass. He felt a twinge in his chest as Michel pulled away, but immediately dismissed it. Tomorrow this would be over and he would sort it all out with Claire.

As he got into his own car he noticed some papers on the ground. Matthieu Mandel's old passport. Lucky he found it. If somebody else had, their whole operation would be compromised. He shoved it into his pocket to dispose of later, and backed his car out of the barn. Joel slid the barn door shut and crawled in beside him.

They followed Michel along the narrow road, slower than they wanted or needed to go. But the weather—and the age of their cars—made driving any faster impossible.

They said nothing. Jean-Jacques was trying to concentrate on the car in front of him and Joel was content to let him do so. But presently Joel noticed a new set of headlights in the distance behind them.

"Look, Jean. They're going to catch up soon."

Jean-Jacques glanced at the lights behind him, trying to think quickly. "There are some farm lanes up here somewhere—I'm sure Michel will take one of them and we can hide in the trees until they've passed."

But Michel didn't.

"I don't think he sees the other car, Joel."

"Can you pass him?"

"I'm afraid that would invite too much attention."

Joel nervously scanned the rear window. The other car was still some distance away, but drawing closer. "Come on, Michel," Jean-

Jacques muttered. But Michel kept driving, the snow caking on his own rear window. "He doesn't see them," Jean-Jacques said. "I'm going to pull off, Joel. I want you to get out and stay in the woods while I try to divert them. I'll come back for you as soon as I can."

But as Jean-Jacques attempted to ease the car off the road, it started to slide. And before he could right it, they had landed on one side—Joel's—in a ditch. Jean-Jacques' head slammed against the steering column; he heard Joel moaning beside him. He struggled to open the door, but gravity worked against him. Before he could budge it, he saw the glint of headlights, close enough now to spot his car. He heard the other car stop. Then there were voices—German voices—and the beam of a flashlight in his face. The door was pried open and he was yanked out of the car, sprawled against it and searched.

The patrol didn't find much—a pen, a few francs, and Matthieu Mandel's passport.

One of the agents held his flashlight to the passport and studied it carefully. Then he handed it to his partner.

"*Juden*," he said.

Erich Braun compared the photograph in the passport to the face of the tall and slender young man before him. He couldn't be sure it was the same man—this one's face was bruised and swelling.

"Where were you going at such a late hour, Monsieur Mandel?"

Jean-Jacques Broussard said nothing.

"Don't you know that Jews aren't permitted to travel after dark?"

Broussard nodded.

"And you deliberately violated this order?"

Again Broussard said nothing. He tried to think. He didn't know what they had done with Joel, and he needed to buy as much time as he could for Michel to escape. If they believed they had Matthieu Mandel here, they wouldn't look for him … and find Claire.

Braun slammed him against the wall. "You must also know that Jews are required to wear the yellow star. Why aren't you wearing yours?" Again, no reply. Braun slapped Broussard's face once, twice, three times. "Where were you going?"

"I don't know," Broussard stammered. "I just wanted to get away …"

"I see. And your friend—he just wanted to get away too?"

He wrapped his massive hand around Broussard's throat. An ugly, oddly shaped scar on Braun's forearm twitched as he squeezed. "Where were you going? Were you meeting someone?"

"No one."

Braun studied Broussard's face. "You don't really look like a Jew, do you?" Broussard met his gaze. "Are you really a Jew?" Braun asked.

"Would any man in his right mind pretend to be?" Broussard replied.

Braun stared for a moment. Then he chuckled and turned to his aides. "A clever Jew," he said, and they all enjoyed the laugh. Then he smacked Broussard's head against the wall, and kicked him in the stomach, ribs and groin until Broussard fell to the floor.

"Jew or no, they're going in the next transport," Braun told an assistant. "Eichmann is furious that we're so far behind in our quotas. I'll start picking them out of nurseries if I have to. I want the orders on my desk ready to sign in the morning."

"*Heil*," the assistant replied.

Braun kicked Broussard again as he was leaving. "*Vive la France*," he said, and laughed.

At the detention camp in Drancy, Jean-Jacques Broussard, now reunited with Joel, was horrified to find so many children—tiny children; infants. "They weren't supposed to take the children," Joel wept. "I thought we'd saved the children."

Erich Braun watched from a platform as internees were crammed into cattle cars. One tall, slender young man caught his eye. "*Adieu, Monsieur Mandel*," he thought.

Broussard stopped to help a woman who had fallen. Rough hands seized him and pushed him away. Broussard turned to face his attacker, a French policeman. Broussard tried to look him in the eye; the policeman refused to look up, but shoved Broussard toward the train.

He and Joel were loaded into the same car. There were so many people in the car … Broussard feared they would all suffocate. His ribs ached, bruised from Erich Braun's boot. And it was cold, so very cold. Still, Broussard was more fortunate than most. He was tall; he could breathe.

"Maman, pick me up," a little girl whimpered. The mother tried to pick her up, but she looked weak, and she could barely move. Jean-Jacques reached for the little girl and hoisted her to his shoulders. "*Merci, Monsieur,*" she said.

"What is your name?"

"Rachel."

"And how old are you?"

Rachel held up four fingers.

Eventually the train lurched forward and began its journey east.

When they reached their destination, Joel and Jean-Jacques were put in one line and Rachel and her mother were sent to another. He never saw her again.

At Auschwitz, they took his shoes, they took his clothes, they took his hair. They gave him a number.

"They're going to know you're not a Jew now," Joel had said as he watched the men ahead of them being paraded past the medical staff. Jean-Jacques had been thinking the same thing. He hoped Matthieu Mandel was out of France by now, and Claire and the others were safe. But he couldn't take the chance. He followed Joel as closely as he could until they got past the doctor, hoping nobody would notice. Nobody did.

He was determined that neither he nor Joel would ever reveal the truth about Matthieu Mandel. He was now #71921; and until he could get home to Chateau-St. Gregoire, Jean-Jacques Broussard was dead.

Gray winter melted into gray summer. Gray summer chilled to gray fall. After the first few weeks, #71921 began to numb to the things he saw. He had been assigned to help in the infirmary, where he had befriended a doctor who had been deported from Antwerp. He quickly discovered which guards he could barter with, and learned to negotiate for extra food or medicines for the patients—a cigarette might be traded for a crust of bread; two for some broth. Lately he had been collecting bits of candles; Hanukkah was approaching, and Dr. Sterner thought a secret observance of the holiday might lift the patients' spirits.

At any moment he could be yanked away from the infirmary and given other tasks. Sometimes he was sent to do the work originally assigned to one of the patients. Sterner warned him that Dr. Mengele had his own reasons for keeping some of the patients alive. To protect his sanity, he would lose himself in dreams of Claire. He imagined the home they would have and the names he would give their children—two boys and a girl would be just right, he thought. Mostly he imagined the moment when he would finally see her again. He had promised to come back. And someday, he *was* going back.

Joel, on the other hand, daily sank further into a haze of hopelessness. He had resisted going with Broussard to the infirmary for the Hanukkah observances until the last night. But as Dr. Sterner lit the last of the candles, Joel told Broussard they were wasting their time. "There is no God," he said, "or if there is, he is not a very good one."

"You can't mean that, Joel," Broussard replied, alarmed. "If you give up on God, you give up on hope!"

Joel smiled and shook his head. "You are a fool, Broussard," he whispered. "There is no hope for us." Joel truly believed that; but something in Broussard's face made him wish he hadn't said it. "I'm sorry, Jean," he said. "If your Jesus can help you through this, then you must cling to him. You must cling to him at all costs."

"*Nes Gadol Hayah Sham*," Dr. Sterner whispered to his patients. "A miracle happened here."

Joel disappeared a few days later. Dodging the guards, Broussard searched through the barracks and grounds, but couldn't find him. Fearing Joel had been sent to the "showers," he ran to the infirmary to see whether Dr. Sterner knew.

"He's gone, Matthieu."

"Gone? Gone where?"

"He asked me to give you this." Sterner handed him a bit of paper. "Please forgive me, Jean," Joel had scrawled. "But they have taken all my other choices away. This choice they will not take from me."

Broussard studied the note for a long time. "What has he done?" he asked.

"He threw himself onto the fence before dawn this morning," Sterner replied. "It was likely the kindest death he could have found here."

"Coward," Broussard whispered, crumpling the note. "Coward!" He punched the wall with his fist.

"Come, Matthieu. You must not hate Joel for what he has done. He is not so young nor resilient as you. Let him go."

Broussard's head drooped. "I don't know how," he said.

"Then start by just letting him go for today. It's a special day for you anyway, isn't it?"

"What?"

"You don't know what day this is?"

"I lose track."

"It's December 25th." Broussard slowly turned to the doctor. "Don't look so surprised, Matthieu. I noticed you weren't Jewish when you arrived, even if Mengele didn't."

"Indeed." He tore Joel's note into tiny bits. "There's nothing special about *this* day. I'd prefer to forget it, if it's all the same to you."

"As you wish." Sterner went about his work, methodically determining which of the patients were desperate enough to get some of the dwindling supply of medications. "Matthieu," he finally said, "I don't know who you really are or how you got here, but I do know this. I used to hear Christians talk about Jesus— the same Christians who pretended not to know me when they came to take me away—but you, you act like Jesus. And we have all of us come to depend on that. If you let that die, you will hurt us all as Joel has hurt you today."

44

Joel's body was taken to the crematorium, just another corpse in that day's quota. Ashes to ashes; dust to dust.

#71921 struggled with the memory of another winter. He had purchased a bouquet of white roses and headed for the church, where he knew he would find Claire helping the children's choir rehearse for the Christmas pageant. He peeked into the sanctuary and saw them all lined up, taller ones behind, the littlest ones in front. And there was Claire in her blue dress, leading them through the carol:

> *Bring a Torch, Jeanette Isabella,*
> *Bring a torch, come hurry and run.*
> *Bring a Torch, Jeanette Isabella,*
> *Bring a torch, to the stable run.*

He caught her eye and dropped one of the roses as he backed out of the sanctuary. Several little girls giggled. He left a trail of roses to the church door, where he waited for the rehearsal to end and Claire to emerge. Finally the music stopped. Claire gathered the roses, one by one—nine, ten, eleven. He waved the last one at her as she approached the door.

How different the world was now. "Oh God please," he begged, "I promised her I'd come back."

On another winter day one year later, the rumors started. Broussard ignored them; there had been rumors before. But then the guards began rounding up the prisoners and marching them out of the camp. Those who were too sick to move were left behind or shot. Sterner hid so that he could stay behind and care for the survivors. Broussard crept around the barracks, leading some of the other prisoners to the infirmary. As he led one to the back of the building, he heard a rifle crack. He felt the frozen ground slap his face. There was shouting, and the pain from the wound in his back made him wince. Nevertheless he pretended to be dead until the shouting, fainter now, subsided. The man he had tried to help lay lifeless beside him. "God please," he begged once more, "please let me keep my promise."

He didn't know how long he lay there, conscious for a little while, swooning for a little while longer. Eventually he heard shouting again, and he was convinced that this time they would make sure he was dead.

But these were not German voices.

There were months in hospitals, letting the wound heal, learning to walk again, asking everybody he saw for news from home. When Jean-Jacques Broussard finally returned to France, Adolf Hitler was dead. Life could begin again.

He had written to Claire to tell her he was coming home. He was not concerned that there had been no reply; mail—everything—was difficult these days.

He couldn't sleep, and the train couldn't go fast enough. He knew he didn't look the same and he hoped she wouldn't mind the cane. But he was going home. And then there would be time to explain everything.

An old woman was selling flowers at the station in Chateau-St. Gregoire, and Broussard instinctively sought a bouquet of white roses. But when he reached into his pocket, he found he only had enough money for one. No matter; as soon as he found work, he would buy her roses every week. He took the rose and headed for Claire's house.

It looked like heaven when it first came into view. But as he drew closer, he saw the house was empty and boarded up. He searched for any sign of life, wondering what to do now.

"Jean-Jacques? Is that you?"

He turned to the street. "Michel?"

"Jean!" They clasped hands and embraced for a moment. "I thought I'd never see you again! Joel …?"

Broussard shook his head. "Do you know where Claire is?"

Michel hesitated for a moment, a strange expression on his face. "Yes," he said, "I'll take you to her."

"Things got very hard after you left," Michel said as they walked, but Broussard only half heard him. They could catch up later. Right now he was concentrating on Claire; he had waited so long.

Then he realized where they were going.

Stunned, he turned on Michel. "Why are you taking me there? What happened?"

Michel looked at Jean for a moment and then to the ground. "One night the Gestapo came and dragged the whole family into the street. She tried to run; one of them shot …"

"You saw this?"

"No. I was in Marseille trying to arrange passage into Spain because we couldn't get into Switzerland anymore. When I got back it was all over. I'm so sorry, Jean."

Broussard's mind raced; his body was limp. "It was quick, Jean. She didn't suffer; I understand many suffered badly," Michel said, looking at Broussard's cane. "Come home with me and let us take care of you."

"Take me to her."

"Why don't you come and rest a little while first?"

"Take me to her."

It was a lonely little space, adorned only with a simple marker in the grass. Broussard knelt beside it and gently pressed Claire's rose into the ground. "What will you do now, Jean?" Michel asked.

Broussard shook his head; his whole life was buried here.

"Well. We can talk about it later. You can stay with Anne and me for a while. You will, won't you?"

Broussard nodded. "Leave me for a little while …"

"All right, Jean. I'll tell Anne you're coming, and then I'll come back for you."

Jean-Jacques Broussard stood alone by Claire's grave, not quite believing or comprehending what was happening to him. He'd never felt so betrayed. Every day since he left Chateau-St. Gregoire he had prayed to keep his promise, and now he was finally home, but for what?

Maybe Joel was right after all. If there was a God, perhaps he was not a very good one.

Jean-Jacques Broussard had always intrigued Philippe Legendre. He had often seen Broussard walk away from lucrative negotiations without a second thought, simply because he was unsure of the other party's motives. It was a habit that not only frustrated other businessmen, but made them that much more eager to do business with Broussard; to be able to boast of a contract with Compagnie St.-Gregoire had become a matter of pride. But Legendre had long suspected that business was just something Broussard did because he did it well, and that on some profoundly personal level, it really didn't matter to him very much.

Across the table, Broussard now sat gently caressing his coffee cup, lost in his long ago sorrow. Philippe waited a moment for him to continue his story, but he was silent.

"And then?"

Broussard glanced at Philippe and straightened in his chair. "Then I became a recluse in Michel's attic and felt sorry for myself. But Michel kept talking about hungry children and men begging for work; and I kept thinking about what Dr. Sterner had said the day Joel died. I started looking for ways to get supplies into the village so the men could repair their homes and the women could feed their children."

"And that's how Compagnie St.-Gregoire got started? To put your village back to work?"

Broussard nodded. "I had seen so much misery. I was determined that so far as I could prevent it, nobody in Chateau-St. Gregoire would ever suffer like that again."

"Did you never think of giving up, like Joel?"

"Of course. But there was no particular honor in dying at Auschwitz. Dying was easy. To survive in spite of them—that was different. And I thought I had something to live for."

"But you never married?"

"When one has lost so much, it is difficult to ever hold so tightly to anything again. I would not permit myself to love anyone else that way. And I can't imagine I would have been an easy man for any woman to live with."

"I suppose that's a safe way to live ... but I should think a rather lonely way."

"Yes. Rather."

"Where is Michel now?"

"He is long dead of a weakened heart."

"What happened to the real Matthieu Mandel? Did he survive?"

"I don't know. I've never had the heart to find out. If he didn't, then it was all for nothing."

Legendre sat straight up in his chair. "No, no, Monsieur Broussard. It wasn't for nothing. You were doing the right thing."

Broussard smiled. "Yes. One must always choose to do the right thing." He gently tapped his fingers on the table. Legendre decided now was as good a time as any to ask the question that had burned in him since he first heard Broussard's name in Gastineau's office.

"I had the impression from Claude Gastineau that you were reluctant to testify against Erich Braun. I don't quite understand—doesn't it matter anymore?"

Broussard's eyes locked on Legendre's. His lips pressed tightly together; the sad smile was gone. "Doesn't it matter?" he said, quietly, evenly. "Every day I must look at the number on my arm and remember how I got it. For 50 years I have stumbled when I walk. I look at my neighbor's children and wonder what my own would have been like—would a boy be tall like me; would a girl have Claire's blue eyes. Make no mistake, Monsieur. It matters every day."

Legendre winced. It had been an honest question; he hadn't meant to offend.

But as quickly as Broussard's anger had flared, it subsided. "Forgive me, Philippe. I should not have spoken to you that way," he said. "I know it isn't easy to understand why I didn't want to be involved. But it's only that I chose a long time ago to follow a higher law; one that commands me to forgive, one that says vengeance belongs to the Lord. Yet I have never wanted to forgive Erich Braun, and after all these years of trying to forget about him, God has thrust him upon me and I don't know *how* to forgive him. I would rather avoid him altogether than forgive him now. I only know that until I do, I am his prisoner still."

Legendre watched Broussard sip the last of his coffee. "Then perhaps this is God's way of telling you he hasn't forgotten Erich Braun, either," he said.

Broussard put down his cup and looked at Legendre. "Perhaps," he replied. Then he reached for his coat. "It's getting late, Philippe, and tomorrow will be a long day. I should be going. Thank you for letting me share your table."

"Thank you for sharing it, Monsieur Broussard. I'll see you tomorrow."

Broussard nodded and left.

Light snow drifted onto Lyon as Jean-Jacques Broussard walked to the inn where he was staying. At the *Palais de Justice* there was a vigil. Some simply held candles while others clung to old photographs or posters with the names, ages and transport numbers of people who had been sent away. Broussard could hear them chanting in the distance. But as he passed an ancient church, it was the singing from inside it that caught his attention. He stopped to listen for a moment.

Angels We Have Heard on High,
Sweetly singing o'er the plain,
And the mountains in reply,
Echoing their joyous strain.

He went to the door, thinking that if he could just sit and listen for a while, the ghosts in his mind would stop rattling their chains.

Gloria, gloria, In Exelcis Deo …

Broussard had stumbled onto a boys' choir rehearsal; he took a seat in the back of the sanctuary. In front was a crèche, and near the altar hung a huge crucifix. Broussard closed his eyes as the choir director coaxed the boys through their next carol.

Bring a Torch, Jeanette Isabella,
Bring a torch, come hurry and run.
Bring a torch, Jeanette Isabella,
Bring a torch, to the stable, run!

"Softly, boys and girls, like a lullaby," Claire said, as she had done a million times before.

It is Jesus, good folk of the village,

Now she was picking up white roses.

Christ is born, and Mary is calling …

Now she was smiling, running toward him, roses filling her arms.

"May I help you, son?"

Jean-Jacques Broussard opened his eyes and looked around. The music had ended, the choir was gone. A middle-aged cleric stood before him, concern in his eyes.

"No, thank you … are you closing?"

"Not yet. The church will be open for prayer a little while longer. You may stay until then, if you wish."

"Thank you."

Broussard sat alone in the sanctuary, grief and dread devouring him. What was it St. Paul had said? "Wretched man that I am! Who will set me free from the body of this death?"

He was drawn to the crucifix; there was no such icon in his church, and he examined this one in its wrenching detail, touching the thorns, the nails; this picture of misery. He closed his eyes against it and turned away, but in his mind he could see it all: the fury of the mob, the blackening skies, the lashes tearing across the young rabbi's body, the mallet smashing against the spikes. He heard the crash of thunder.

And the voices—all those voices grappling together for his mind.

"Are you the king of the Jews?"

"Where were you going, Monsieur Mandel?"

"Crucify him!"

"Come back, Jean, Please come back."

"Everyone who is of the truth hears My voice."

"What is truth?"

"You don't really look like a Jew, do you?"

"You are a fool, Broussard. There is no hope for us."

"My God, my God! Why have you forsaken me?"

"You must always choose to do the right thing, Alexandre."

"Father, forgive them, for they know not what they do."

"It is too much," Broussard whispered.

"It is finished," said the Lord.

Jean-Jacques Broussard sank to the floor, his whole body shaking as he wept. He wept for Claire, he wept for Joel, he wept for little Rachel. He wept for Jesus on the cross.

He wept for the life he had planned and the life he had known.

"My God, what you ask is so hard," he pleaded. "I have no will to forgive this man. If I must do this thing, you will have to help me.

"All these years I tried to accept my fate and go on, convincing myself that it was somehow what you wanted, and I never dared to ask you why. But the question has always been there, every moment, preying on my mind. You could have stopped it. Why didn't you? Why?

"Can it be that you wanted me to know a little of what you suffered? Or did you know I needed to?"

"It's nearly time, Claude. Where is Broussard?"

"I told him 9 o'clock, sir. It's five minutes till."

"This presiding judge doesn't give second chances, Claude. If Broussard doesn't show up, we either give up the case, or start all over with a new trial."

"He'll be here, sir." Claude Gastineau looked François Fournier square in the face. Fournier frowned and looked away. Gastineau glanced nervously at the door. A moment later he heard uneven footsteps in the corridor; Broussard appeared in the doorway. He looked back at Fournier. "Thank God," Fournier mumbled, and gathered up his documents. Gastineau allowed himself a sigh, carefully hiding it from Fournier.

Philippe Legendre watched Jean-Jacques Broussard as the man they called Erich Braun was wheeled into his place behind a bulletproof box. Whatever Broussard was feeling, he did not show it. *How does he do that?* Legendre wondered.

Broussard told the court about the snow and the wreck and Matthieu Mandel's passport; about Rachel and Joel, about the train and the barracks and the ovens. He told them how Erich Braun had beaten him and signed the papers for his deportation. He told them about the scar on Erich Braun's arm; he showed them the number on his own. Philippe Legendre felt his flesh crawl.

Claude Gastineau led Jean-Jacques Broussard to the box where the man on trial was sitting. A guard held his arm up to the glass, revealing the scar. Broussard trembled. The defendant refused to look up.

"Is this the man who beat you at the Gestapo office?"

Broussard took in the wheelchair, the hollow cheeks, the withered face. The eyes, still cold and distant. This was indeed Erich Braun, there was no question about that. But clearly he was not the same man he had been in 1943. And now, all Broussard felt toward him was pity.

"Will you not even look at me?" Broussard asked.

"Monsieur Broussard," Gastineau whispered.

"I want to be sure," Broussard said.

Braun looked straight into Broussard's eyes. "Mandel," he said. "I knew you were no Jew."

Philippe Legendre heard gasps all around as his own mouth dropped open. François Fournier tried to hide his delight. Stunned, Claude Gastineau wasn't sure what to do. The presiding judge demanded decorum as spectators began to shout at Braun.

Jean-Jacques Broussard quietly asked Gastineau whether he could be dismissed now.

Philippe Legendre opted for a back door to avoid the cameras and chaos in front of the *Palais de Justice*. Let the broadcasters have their moment; he'd had his last night.

In the shadows he could see Jean-Jacques Broussard, obviously wanting to avoid the crush as well. His jagged steps echoed down the hall as Legendre caught up with him.

"Where are you going now?" Legendre asked.

"I'm going home, Philippe."

"You don't want to stay for the mopping up?"

"We both know what will happen, Philippe. He will be sent to a prison or a hospital and either way, he will die a prisoner of France. There's no point in my lingering here."

"He convicted himself, Monsieur Broussard. He's earned his own consequences. There's nothing for you to be sorry for." Broussard smiled. "Have you forgiven him?" Legendre asked.

"I don't hate him anymore," Broussard said. "I suppose that's a start."

They walked together down the long corridor. Outside, the sunlight was fading fast.

"May I ask you one more question, Monsieur?"

"One more, Philippe."

"How many people were you able to smuggle out of France before you were caught?"

Broussard smiled. "Not enough," he whispered. He offered Legendre his hand. "*Au revoir*, Philippe."

"*Au revoir*," Philippe answered, and watched Jean-Jacques Broussard disappear into the street.

Madeleine Villon bit her lip as she read Philippe Legendre's article in *Le Monde*. She had known her gentle neighbor so long and so well; he had employed her husband and befriended her children. How could she have missed this? She folded the paper and put it away for Alain to read when he got home—if he hadn't seen it already.

But indeed he had. In the cafe, in the market and certainly at Compagnie-St. Gregoire, people talked of nothing else. There was a mix of pride and sadness in their conversation; pride because he was *their* Monsieur Broussard, this secret hero of the Resistance. Sadness because they hadn't known about this defining episode of his life. But wasn't it just like Monsieur Broussard not to trouble anyone with his own struggles?

Madeleine was coaxing Lisette into bed when Lisette noticed the lights were on in Monsieur Broussard's house.

"Look, Maman! Monsieur Broussard's come home! Could I go and see him tomorrow?"

"I think we should wait a few days, Lisette. Monsieur Broussard has had a busy trip; I'm sure he's very tired. Come and say your prayers now."

Lisette folded her little hands and asked the Lord to bless Maman, Papa, Monsieur Broussard and even Alexandre. Madeleine looked out the window at Monsieur Broussard's house, and spotted him standing by his own window, lighting candles.

Of course. Hanukkah.

A dozen squirming children surrounded Madeleine as she tried to wrestle her own two into their choir robes for the Christmas pageant. Alexandre said the collar was strangling him and refused to fasten the snap at the top. Lisette had no such qualms, but her robe was a bit long. "You'll have to hold it up a little when you go up the stairs, Lisette, or you may trip over it. Alexandre, you help her, all right?"

"Yes ma'am."

In Pastor Duvalier's study, Jean-Jacques Broussard accepted the coffee Duvalier offered. "Why didn't you tell me about all this, Jean?" Duvalier asked.

"There was nothing you could do, Pierre. I saw no reason to bother you with it."

"I could have gone with you; and at the very least, I could have prayed for you."

Broussard laughed. "Forgive me, but prayer was the last thing I wanted; though it was probably the thing I needed most."

"I can't pretend to know why God allows the things he does," Duvalier said, "but I know there must be a reason. And I know that one day he'll tell us."

They heard the children lining up in the hall. "Well. It's time," Broussard said, handing Duvalier his cup and heading for the door.

"Jean …"

Broussard stopped at the door.

"You'll see her again some day. You believe that, don't you?"

Broussard looked at Duvalier for a long moment. "I have to believe it," he said.

Madeleine Villon was on her way to the sanctuary when she noticed an older man and a young boy—about 13—standing in the foyer looking lost. "Madame," the man said, "I'm looking for Jean-Jacques Broussard; I was told I might find him here. Do you know if he's here?"

Like everyone else in Chateau-St. Gregoire, Madeleine was feeling keenly protective of her old friend. "May I tell him who's looking for him?" she asked.

"Matthieu Mandel."

Madeleine froze.

Monsieur Broussard brushed past Madeleine and approached the man in the foyer. "I am Jean-Jacques Broussard," he said, peering into the man's face. They stood like that for a moment, studying each other, looking for recognition in each other's faces. Madeleine knew she should leave, but she couldn't move.

"This is my grandson, Jacob," Mandel said, a single tear dripping down his face. "We have traveled here from Bern to see you. I never got the chance to thank you before."

"Hello, Jacob," Broussard said, taking the boy's hand. Mandel handed Broussard a photograph. "This is the rest of my family," he said. There was Mandel, and a woman who must have been his wife, three younger couples and a considerable cluster of children. "Every winter I light the candles and I tell them about the war and the soldiers and the kindness of a stranger. But until now, I never knew who you were, or what my life had cost you." He smiled a little. "You see, I still read the French papers."

Pastor Duvalier appeared and touched Broussard's shoulder. "We need to get started, Jean."

"I'm coming," Broussard said. Duvalier nodded and left.

"We've come at a bad time," Mandel said.

"Not at all. You may stay for the service, if you wish, and afterward perhaps you'll tell me about your family." Broussard handed the photograph back to Mandel. "I'm very glad to see you again, Monsieur Mandel," he said as he left. "Very glad."

"Come and sit with my husband and me, Monsieur Mandel," Madeleine said, finally finding her voice. "Our children are singing in the choir."

There was silence in the sanctuary as Jean-Jacques Broussard stood for the Scripture reading. It was the first time most in the congregation had seen him since he had testified at Erich Braun's trial. He felt their eyes on him as he opened his Bible to the Christmas story in St. Luke's gospel. He looked out at them, friends, employees, neighbors; and Matthieu and Jacob Mandel seated with Alain and Madeleine Villon. All of them huddled together in the candlelight, watching him, expectant. There was something he needed to say to them. He turned to another passage. And, with only the slightest quiver in his voice, he began to read.

"From the third chapter of the Book of Ecclesiastes:

"To everything there is a season, and a time to every purpose under heaven:

"A time to be born, and a time to die; a time to plant, and a time to uproot what is planted.

"A time to kill, and a time to heal; A time to tear down, and a time to build up.

"A time to weep, and a time to laugh; A time to mourn, and a time to dance.

"A time to throw stones, and a time to gather stones together. A time to embrace, and a time to refrain from embracing.

"A time to search, and a time to give up as lost; A time to keep, and a time to cast away.

"A time to tear apart, and a time to sew together; A time to be silent, and a time to speak.

"A time to love, and a time to hate;

"A time for war, and a time for peace.

"… God has made everything beautiful in his time."

Jean-Jacques Broussard took his seat next to Pastor Duvalier as the children began their processional. "That was an unusual Christmas passage, Jean," Duvalier whispered.

"It has been an unusual season," Broussard replied. Little Lisette Villon, blond curls dangling around her face, smiled and waved at Broussard as the children filed past. Alexandre tried to hurry her along.

Duvalier studied the familiar, unknowable man seated next to him. "*Joyeux Noel*, Jean," he said.

Broussard winked at Lisette. "*Joyeux Noel*," he replied, and leaned back to soak in the children's sweetly discordant voices as they filled the sanctuary and spilled into the blackness settling on Chateau-St. Gregoire:

> *Bring a Torch, Jeanette Isabella,*
> *Bring a torch, come hurry and run,*
> *Bring a torch, Jeanette Isabella,*
> *Bring a torch, to the stable, run!*

It is Jesus, good folk of the village,
Christ is born and Mary is calling,
Ah, ah, beautiful is the Mother,
Ah, ah, beautiful is the Son!

Made in the USA
Middletown, DE
08 December 2022

17518393R00040